RACING ACE

Build It! Jump It!

Written by
Larry Dane Brimner

Illustrated by
Kaylani Juanita

ACORN™
SCHOLASTIC INC.

To the Mogan crew: Quinn, Maddy, and Ruby. — LDB

I dedicate this book to the three kids at the skate park
who encouraged me to drop into the bowl. Though I can't
remember your names, I remember your cheers
when I rolled in without falling. — KJ

Library of Congress Cataloging-in-Publication Data
Names: Brimner, Larry Dane, author. | Juanita, Kaylani, illustrator.
Title: Build it! Jump it! / written by Larry Dane Brimner ; illustrated by
Kaylani Juanita.
Description: New York : Acorn/Scholastic Inc., (2022) | Series: Racing Ace; 2 |
Audience: Ages 4–6. | Audience: Grades K–1. | Summary: Ace builds
her own skateboard, but it takes a lot of practice (and some falls) to
learn to skate well—and then she builds a ramp and takes it to the park
to skate with her new skateboarding friends.
Identifiers: LCCN 2020001060 | ISBN 9781338553802 (paperback) | ISBN
9781338553819 (library binding) |
Subjects: LCSH: Skateboarding—Juvenile fiction. | Skateboards—Juvenile
fiction. | CYAC: Skateboarding—Fiction. | Skateboards—Fiction.
Classification: LCC PZ7.B767 Bu 2021 | DDC (E)—dc23
LC record available at https://lccn.loc.gov/2020001060

10 9 8 7 6 5 4 3 2 1   22 23 24 25 26

Printed in China   62

First edition, June 2022
Edited by Katie Carella
Book design by Maria Mercado

WHEELS

This is Ace.
She likes to race.

This is Ace's new board.
She cannot wait to finish it.

Ace looks for something.

Where is it?

Ace opens a big, brown box.

Here it is!

This is what Ace was looking for.

Now Ace can get to work.

Ace puts on her goggles.

She drills holes into her board.

Ace needs something else now.

She knows where she left it.

The bag is in her backpack.

The wheels are in the bag.

Ace loves wheels.

Wheels roll.

They spin.

They go.

Ace likes to go, go, go.

She adds the wheels to her board.

She tightens the nuts.

She turns the bolts.

Something is missing. But what?

Ace knows what is missing.

She adds a sticker to her board.

Then she adds another one.

There! Ace's skateboard is perfect.

Now Ace must get ready.

She puts on her helmet.

She puts on her pads.

Ready! Set!

Let's skate!

UPS AND DOWNS

Ace takes her board to the park.
Two other skaters are there.

Skating looks easy.
Just get on and roll.

Ace looks at her skateboard.
Can she do it?

She plops her skateboard down.

She pushes off.

Ace rolls down the sidewalk.
Go, Ace! Go, go, go!

Uh-oh!

Oh no!

OOF!

Skating is not easy.

Ace gets up.
She dusts herself off.

Now Ace starts to go faster,

and faster,

and faster.

She is going way too fast.

Look out for the dog, Ace!

Turn! Turn! Turn!

Oh no.
Ace is down again.

Try again, Ace. Don't quit.
It takes time to learn how to skate.

Take it slow. Take it easy.
Stay steady, Ace. That's it.

Ace, you are a pro!

UP, UP, AND AWAY

Ace has a big idea.
She will build something new.

She drills.

She saws.

She hammers.

Ace builds, and builds, and builds.

Wow, Ace! That ramp is amazing.

Ace is ready to test it out.

She puts on her pads.

She tugs the strap to make her helmet snug.

Ace rolls over the wood.

CLACK-CLACK!
CLACK-CLACK!
CLACK-CLACK!

She pops.

She hops.

She spins.

Then she has a new idea.

Ace skates to the park.
Where are her skater friends?

There they are.
It's time to test out the ramp together!

The skaters drop
down into Ace's ramp.

They shoot up
the other side.

They fly up, up, and away.

Ace wants to catch air, too.

Ace races down one side of the ramp.

She starts up the other side.

She slides backward on the ramp.

Almost, Ace.

That is what the pads are for.

She gets up to try again.
You've got this, Ace.

Go, Ace! You can do it.
Yes, you can.

She rockets up the other side.
That's catching air, Ace.

ABOUT THE CREATORS

LARRY DANE BRIMNER

lives in Tucson, Arizona, where he mountain bikes, jogs, and roller-skates when he is not writing. He has tried to skateboard, but it wasn't a pretty sight. He wishes he had thought to belt a big pillow around his middle so he would have had something soft to land on.

KAYLANI JUANITA

does not know how to skateboard, but she does know how to roller-skate. She owns a pair of orange suede skates with yellow heart-shaped stoppers. One summer at the skatepark, she collided with her husband while he was skateboarding. You can still see the scar from her elbow scrape to this day.

YOU CAN DRAW ACE!

1 Draw Ace's body.

2 Add face details. Draw Ace's shirt and shorts.

3 Add Ace's helmet, elbow pads, and knee pads.

4 Add her hair. Draw socks and sneakers on her feet.

5 Give Ace a skateboard.

6 Color in your drawing!

WHAT'S YOUR STORY?

Ace builds a ramp so she can catch air.
Imagine **you** join Ace on her ramp.
Would you be steady on your feet?
Who would catch more air—you or Ace?
Write and draw your story!